STORM SURFER

BY JAKE MADDOX

illustrated by Tuesday Mourning

text by Lisa Trumbauer

Librarian Reviewer
Chris Kreie
Media Specialist, Eden Prairie Schools, MN
MS in Information Media, St. Cloud State University, MN

Reading Consultant
Mary Evenson
Middle School Teacher, Edina Public Schools, MN
MA in Education, University of Minnesota

STONE ARCH BOOKS Hudson, IL 61748
Minneapolis San Diego

Impact Books are published by Stone Arch Books
151 Good Counsel Drive, P.O. Box 669
Mankato, Minnesota 56002
www.stonearchbooks.com

Library of Congress Cataloging-in-Publication Data
Maddox, Jake.
    Storm Surfer / by Jake Maddox; illustrated by Tuesday Mourning.
    p. cm. — (Impact Books — A Jake Maddox Sports Story)
    ISBN 978-1-4342-0471-4 (library binding)
    ISBN 978-1-4342-0521-6 (paperback)
    [1. Surfing—Fiction. 2. Self-confidence—Fiction.] I. Mourning,
Tuesday, ill. II. Title.
PZ7.M25643Sto 2008
[Fic]—dc22   2007031263

Summary: Jill never thought her week at surf camp would be
interrupted by a hurricane, but one is heading for the North Carolina
coast. She knows to stay away from the water when a storm is coming.
But Abby and Sara think surfing in a hurricane will be amazing.
Who will save them when the waves get out of control? Wes, the local
guy whose waves the girls always steal? Jill, who they pushed off her
surfboard? Or Meg, who can barely stand on her board? Time is
running out, and the storm is coming. . . .

Art Director: Heather Kindseth
Graphic Designer: Kay Fraser

1 2 3 4 5 6 13 12 11 10 09 08

TABLE OF CONTENTS

Chapter 1 >
SHARK GIRL

Jill scanned the ocean. Her legs dangled over the sides of her surfboard. Her board bobbed gently in the water. She was looking for a wave, any wave, that would take her in to shore.

The ocean was way too calm. Definitely not a good surfing day.

Suddenly, a shrill scream burst across the water.

"Shark!"

Jill quickly turned on her board. She looked in the direction of the warning. Then she shook her head.

"Not again," she said to herself. She lay down on her board and began paddling.

"Shark!" Meg shouted. She waved her arms frantically. "It's not a mistake this time! I swear!"

"Meg!" Jill called to her. She was still several feet away. "You really have to stop."

Jill could tell that Meg was panicked. Her eyes were wide, and her legs were drawn up on her board, her knees up to her chin.

She stopped waving when she saw Jill, and she gripped the edge of her surfboard. Jill could see that Meg's knuckles were bone white.

Jill paddled up to her. "You know the story of the boy who cried wolf, right? You're going to be known as the girl who cried shark!" she said.

Meg released a shaky hand from her board. She pointed over Jill's shoulder. "Look!"

Jill looked where Meg pointed. At first, she didn't see anything. Then she caught a glimpse of something. Something that looked a bit like a shark's fin.

"Stay here," she told Meg. "I'll be right back."

Jill paddled her surfboard toward the finlike thing. Two other objects poked up around it. They looked circular. They looked suspiciously like the tubes of snorkel gear.

Jill drifted up to one and placed her hand over the top of the tube. Within seconds, a head came spluttering to the surface. "Hey! What did you do that for?" It was Abby Miller. And Jill was sure the other snorkel belonged to Sara Roberts.

Sure enough, Sara's blond head popped up from the water. "We were just having a little fun," Sara said.

"That girl is so afraid of sharks, she'll believe anything is deadly," Abby added.

"Even a surfboard!" Sara said, giggling.

Jill rolled her eyes. "Whatever," she said.

She watched as Abby and Sara flipped the surfboard over, hiding its fake fin. Abby lunged onto it, lay on her stomach, and began paddling toward shore. Sara swam swiftly beside her.

Jill turned her own board around and headed back to Meg. The scared girl still sat glued to her surfboard.

"See?" Jill said. "No shark."

"How did you know that?" Meg asked.

Jill shrugged. "Shark fins are usually much, much bigger."

Meg's eyes widened.

Jill laughed. "I'm kidding! I could just tell it wasn't a shark. It looked more like the bottom of a surfboard. Come on. Let's go in. The ocean is dead today."

Jill watched Meg untuck her knees and stretch her legs out along the board.

"Do I have to put my feet in the water? You know, a surfboard looks just like a seal to a shark," Meg said.

Jill smiled. "You watch the nature channel too much."

Meg finally smiled back, weakly. "Yeah, well, what can I say? I like to research something before I do it."

The two girls started paddling to shore.

"So why are you at surf camp, if you're terrified of the ocean?" Jill asked.

"I'm not afraid of the ocean. I'm just afraid of sharks," Meg said.

"Well, North Carolina might not be the surfing capital of the world, but I don't think you have to worry about sharks here," Jill told her. She smiled as they walked onto the beach.

"Famous last words!" Meg said.

Chapter 2 ›
THE IDEA

"Everyone! Time to sign up for the camp competition!" Krista said, clapping her hands.

Krista was one of the camp instructors. Tall, thin, tan, and blond, she looked like a surfer girl.

Jill and Meg grasped their surfboards under their arms and jogged up the beach. About a dozen other kids gathered around Krista.

Krista stood in front of a wooden booth. The booth looked like a huge lemonade stand. Across the top, instead of "Lemonade for Sale," the sign read "Surf Camp."

That afternoon, an extra banner flew from the stand. "Camp Competition" flapped in the ocean breeze.

Jill sighed. The competition was for teams of two. She and her best friend, Mia, had planned to attend surf camp together. Mia's parents decided at the last minute to take a family vacation. Jill had made plenty of friends during surf camp, but most of the kids were already paired up.

This was Jill's third summer at the camp. It was supposed to be the summer she and Mia finally won the competition. Now it looked like she'd have to sit it out.

She saw Abby and Sara in front of the sign-up line, giggling. Of course they were going to enter. They'd probably win, too.

They weren't the best surfers, but they were the bravest. And sometimes, they were the craziest. Suddenly, Jill had an idea. She turned to Meg.

Meg was busy twisting her long blond hair to get all the water out. "I'm so glad we don't have to enter the competition if we don't want to," Meg said. "I think I'll just watch from shore."

Jill grabbed Meg's arm and pulled her toward the stand. "I don't think so," Jill said.

"What do you mean?" Meg asked.

"You and me!" Jill said. "We're going to be a team. And we're going to win!"

The next day, Jill and Meg waded into the ocean. Their surfboards floated in front of them.

"This is a total mistake," Meg said. "I'm a disaster."

"Tell me again why you signed up for surf camp?" Jill asked.

"I didn't," Meg explained. "My parents signed me up because I'm on my swim team at school."

"So you like the water," Jill said.

"I do! But I like it in a pool with chlorine and no rocks and no surprises," Meg said, shaking her head.

"I've been swimming these beaches all my life," Jill said. "You won't find many surprises in North Carolina either."

"What about riptides? And crabs in the sand? And huge waves?" Meg looked worried.

Jill laughed. "I wish we could catch a huge wave!" she exclaimed. "We'd win this competition for sure!"

The water lapped around their knees. "Seriously," Jill said. "Surfing's not all that hard. All you need is a double dose of C."

"The sea?" Meg asked.

"No, the letter C," Jill explained. "Confidence and courage."

"I don't think I have much of either of those," Meg said.

"Don't worry," Jill told her. "We won't go out as far as we did yesterday. We'll only go out waist high. That should build your confidence."

"What about the courage part?" Meg asked.

Jill smiled. "That part will come with practice," she said.

Meg frowned. "Can't we practice on shore, like we did before?" she asked.

"I don't think sand surfing is a sport," Jill said, smiling. "But if it was, you'd be an expert."

Meg returned Jill's smile, but it wasn't a big one.

Jill pushed herself up onto her board and lay flat on her stomach. "Okay, start by getting on the board, like I just did," she said.

Meg slid onto the board. "That's easy," she said. "That's always the easy part."

"Good. Now, push yourself up and swing your feet onto the board, like this." Jill showed Meg how to land on the board with one foot slightly ahead of the other.

Meg tried to copy her. Instead of landing on her feet, she fell on her knees. The board wobbled, and then it toppled over, taking Meg with it.

Meg splashed back up to the surface. "What am I doing wrong?" she asked.

Jill straddled the board, her legs hanging over the sides. "You're landing on your knees first, not your feet," she explained. "That can throw your balance off."

"Okay, let me try again," Meg said.

The girls practiced for an hour. Krista came over a few times to offer advice. Jill didn't even think of letting Meg try to catch a wave. She had to be able to stand on the board first.

They stayed in the shallow part of the beach. Farther down, Jill saw the more expert surfers doing their stuff.

She held back a sigh. She wanted to be there. She wanted to catch a wave. She wanted to feel the power of the water beneath her. But she wouldn't leave her new partner.

Still studying the surfers, Jill narrowed her eyes. Something was off. She'd seen something that just wasn't supposed to be done.

"Come on," she said to Meg. She flipped onto her board and began paddling across the water.

"Jill, wait!" Meg called after her. "What's wrong?"

"Abby and Sara!" Jill said over her shoulder. She paddled harder.

Chapter 4 >
THE RULES

By the time they reached the group, the argument was full blown. Abby and Sara stood on the beach, surfboards under their arms.

Two guys and another girl stood in front of them. All of them were dripping wet. One surfboard lay in the sand.

"We did not steal your wave!" Abby said to a guy in long, colorful swim trunks. "You were just too slow."

Jill recognized the guy. His name was Wes, and he didn't go to surf camp. He was a local. He was a few years older than they were. Jill had seen him the summers before. They'd talked a few times.

"The two of you cut me off," Wes said. His brown hair dripped into his eyes.

"We didn't cut you off," Sara said.

Abby nodded. "Yeah," she said.

"Yes, you did," Jill said, stepping up to the group.

All their heads turned to her. Abby squinted and said, "What do you know about it? You weren't even here."

"I saw you from down the beach," Jill explained. "You broke surfing rule number one."

"Surfing doesn't have rules," Sara said.

"Not officially," Jill said. "But everyone knows that you give respect to the more experienced surfers. You never steal another surfer's wave."

"We're experienced!" Abby said angrily.

"And we did not steal this guy's wave!" Sara added.

Jill shrugged. "That's not how I saw it," she said. "And I bet that's not how they saw it. Right?" She looked at the girl and the guy standing next to Wes. All three of them nodded.

"See?" Jill said, turning back to Abby and Sara.

"What are you, the surfing police?" Abby asked.

Jill smiled and said, "Hardly! But we don't want to give the surfing camp a bad name."

Abby and Sara had run out of words. They stared at Jill a moment longer, then quickly walked off with their surfboards under their arms.

"That was awesome!" Meg said, standing behind Jill. "Did you really see them cut this guy off?"

Jill nodded. "Sorry about Abby and Sara," she said to Wes and his friends. "We're not all like that at surf camp."

"Usually not," Wes said. "You're Jill, right? Didn't we meet last summer?"

"That's right," Jill said. "Good memory!"

"Don't apologize for your friends," Wes said.

"They're not our friends," Meg said.

"They still should show respect," Jill said. "Those two are always trying to make other people look stupid."

"That's why we're going to beat them in the camp competition," Meg said.

Wes laughed. "Really? I saw you guys down the beach. You can't even stand up!"

Meg frowned. "I know. Jill's a pro. And she's really patient. I'm not a bad swimmer. I'm on my swim team at my neighborhood pool. I just can't get the hang of surfing."

"There's nothing to it!" Wes said. "You just have to feel the ocean. Pretend the ocean is your friend."

"I think that's the problem," Jill said. "Meg thinks the ocean is full of things out to get her, like sharks."

"And jellyfish! And stingrays!" Meg shouted.

Wes and his friends burst out laughing.

"See what I mean?" Jill said.

"I've got the perfect solution," Wes said. "We'll have you up on a surfboard in no time."

Chapter 5 ›
SPECIAL TRAINING

"A swimming pool?" Meg said the next day. "You're kidding, right?"

"I never kid about surfing," Wes said.

"It's perfect!" Jill agreed. "I don't know why I didn't think of it before."

They had arranged to meet Wes at a nearby water park first thing in the morning, before the park opened. Surfboards were not allowed in the park, of course, but Wes's uncle was the manager.

When Wes explained the situation, his uncle agreed to let them in before the park opened.

Meg looked skeptically at the pool. Her surfboard was propped up against a nearby table. "I feel safer in the pool, but I don't know about this," she said.

"We only have half an hour," Wes said. "But I think that's enough time to get you used to the feel of the board underneath your feet."

"You think so?" Meg asked nervously. She looked at Jill.

"You like the pool, right?" Jill said. "Now we're just combining the pool with a surfboard."

"And before you know it, you'll be surfing with the best of them," Wes said.

"Why do you care if I can surf or not?" Meg asked Wes.

Wes shrugged. "Let's just say I'd like to see those other two girls put in their place," he said.

* * *

After half an hour, Meg was able to stand on her surfboard. She'd even ridden a few waves, made by Jill and Wes moving their hands in the water.

Jill thought Meg had done pretty well. She was a good swimmer, at least when she wasn't worried about being eaten by sharks. When she fell into the water — which was often — her strokes were smooth and strong. Jill noticed that Meg didn't hesitate to get wet or put her head under water. In fact, she seemed like a natural.

Now all they had to do was get Meg used to the ocean.

Jill and Meg thanked Wes and left him at the park. They wanted to get back to camp before anyone realized they'd been gone. Or before anyone realized what they'd been doing.

Jill just didn't want anyone to know about Meg's extra training, especially Abby and Sara.

Jill and Meg walked from the main street onto the beach. As they got closer to camp, they could see that about two dozen kids were standing around the surf camp stand. Krista stood behind it, talking.

When they got closer, Jill realized something was wrong. Krista was talking slowly. She was not her usual bubbly self.

"What's going on?" Jill said, nudging one of the guys in their group.

"Hurricane," Cal whispered back. "Looks like we'll be grounded in a few days."

"Hurricane?" Meg said. "When?"

"It's down the coast, in Florida," Cal told her. "It's supposed to be here by Friday. It's not a big one, so we don't have to leave the coast, but still."

"Friday!" Jill said. "But that's—"

"That's right, Jill," Krista said loudly. "That's the day of the competition. Nice of you and Meg to show up this morning."

Chapter 6 ›
A BEAUTY

Twenty heads turned to look at Jill and Meg. Jill felt heat crawl up her face. She didn't like to attract attention, especially negative attention. Now she'd have to come up with an excuse for why they were late.

But Meg spoke up. "We're sorry, Krista," she said. "Jill was just giving me some extra pointers down the beach. She didn't want anyone to see how bad I was."

"That's not hard," Abby said loudly.

"If you girls had been on time, you would have heard that we're going to have to postpone the surfing competition," Krista said. She sounded annoyed.

"For how long?" Jill asked.

"As I was just explaining," Krista said, "it's hard to tell. Hurricanes can be very unpredictable. We know it's coming up the coast, and we know it's going to hit North Carolina. We don't know how strong it will be, and we don't know where, exactly, it will land."

"I think it's exciting," Cal said. "The waves during a hurricane are awesome!"

"And dangerous," Krista said. "Once we put up the red flags, I don't want to see anyone surfing. In fact, you shouldn't even be near the water. Is that understood?"

Everyone nodded.

"Good," Krista said. "Now, for those of you who have already mastered how to find and catch a wave, let's work on angling and leaning. The rest of you will work with Jon on perfecting the basics."

Jill looked longingly at the advanced group of surfers. She could handle the basic stuff in her sleep. But she didn't want to leave Meg.

It was as if Meg were reading her mind. "You should go with them, Jill," Meg said with a nervous smile. "I'll be fine with the basics class. At least I can stand up on the board now, right?"

Jill was torn. "Are you sure?" she asked. "You're probably in better hands with Jon than with me at this point."

Meg nodded. "Since the competition is postponed, I'll have time to practice more. And you should, too."

Jill didn't hesitate. "Remember what we did at the pool!" she said. Then she sprinted away. "You'll be great!" she called back.

Jill liked helping Meg, but as she ran toward the advanced class, she felt free. She dashed into the ocean after the other surfers and slapped her board on top of the water. She threw herself onto her board and paddled toward the small group.

Suddenly, she saw it. A wave. A wonderful, beautiful wave.

It would roll right by the class. Her fellow surfers were sitting on their boards, listening to Krista. They would miss it.

But it would reach her just in time.

Jill turned her board around and pointed it toward shore. She began paddling, moving with the motion of the wave, waiting until she could feel it under her. She would wait until she sensed that it was just the right moment.

One more second. One more second.

Now!

Jill pushed herself up on her board. She put out her arms to steady herself and angled her feet to maintain her balance. She could feel the power of the wave. The wind and spray whipped around her.

Out of the corner of her eye, Jill saw a flash of movement. A second later, something hurtled into her.

Jill flew off her board.

Chapter 7 ›
WIPEOUT!

Jill knew how to fall. She just didn't like doing it.

She covered her head and dove into the water. She felt the wave pummel her, but the worst part of the wave had already passed. Something tugged her foot, so she knew her surfboard was still attached to its leash cord.

That was good. It would be awful to lose it. It was one of her favorite things.

Lifting her head, she broke the surface of the water. She looked around, trying to spot what had knocked her off her board.

Abby and Sara were high-fiving down on the beach. Jill pulled her surfboard toward her, hopped on, and swam to shore.

"Nice ride!" she heard Sara tell Abby.

"It was a great ride until you ran into me, you mean," Jill said.

"Was that you?" Abby asked innocently. "I didn't even notice."

"Jill! Are you all right?" Wes called as he walked over. He had been surfing down the beach when Abby and Sara crashed into Jill.

"I'm fine," Jill assured him. "It probably looked worse than it was."

"It looked pretty bad from where we were," Sara said.

"That was a pretty big wipeout," Abby said.

"That didn't look like a wipeout to me," Wes said. He looked suspiciously at Abby and Sara. "From where I was standing, it looked like someone knocked Jill off her board," he added.

Abby and Sara giggled softly.

Wes turned to Abby and Sara. "You wouldn't know anything about that, would you?" he asked.

"Us?" Abby said innocently. "Nope, we were just surfing. We weren't paying any attention to Jill."

Then Jon, the basics instructor, walked up. He looked angry.

"Did you run into Jill?" Jon asked, crossing his arms.

"Of course not," Sara said.

"We wouldn't be congratulating each other if we'd run over someone, would we?" Abby added.

Jon stared at them. Jill thought he believed them. "You girls be careful," he said finally.

"Oh, we will, Jon, honest," Abby said.

Jill watched him walk down the beach. She planned to tell Abby and Sara just what she thought, but she didn't want to do it in front of an instructor.

When she turned back to Abby and Sara, though, they were gone. They were in the ocean again.

Their legs hung over each side of their boards, and they leaned forward, talking to each other. Jill could only guess what they were saying.

"Trying to figure out another way to make our lives miserable, probably," she said to Wes.

"No kidding," he said. "I'm glad you're okay. I have to go. See you later."

Jill looked at Abby and Sara again. They liked to make trouble, that was for sure. But they also liked to do their own thing. And Jill knew that when it came to surfing, that could be dangerous. Very dangerous.

Now, she just needed to figure out what their next move was.

Chapter 8 >
RED FLAGS

Friday morning dawned beautiful and sunny.

If the television in the common room hadn't been constantly set to the weather channel, no one would have known the hurricane was coming.

"Radar doesn't lie," Cal said, slouched on a couch along with a few other kids.

Jill and Meg sat on the other sofa. Abby and Sara weren't around.

"Why couldn't it have gone farther into the ocean?" Jill said. "The way this thing is heading, the Carolina coast is going to be right in the middle of it."

"I hate to admit that I'm glad," Meg said.

Everyone turned to stare at her.

"I mean, I'm totally horrible at surfing. I need all the practice time I can get before the competition," Meg said quietly.

"You just need confidence," Jill said. "And courage. In fact, come on. Let's go build up some confidence and courage and watch the storm come in."

The girls jumped up from the couch and walked outside. Although the sun was out, Jill could feel the change in the air as the hurricane came closer.

The wind had picked up a bit, blowing her hair around her face. And the air felt heavy, pushed down by the pressure from the storm.

* * *

By that afternoon, the hurricane was almost upon them.

"Look at the size of those waves!" Wes said as they stood on the beach.

Only a few hours before, the ocean had been fairly calm. It hadn't even been windy.

Now, Jill watched the water rise, like the claws of a bear or a dragon, then thunder down onto the beach. As soon as one wave broke, another wave rose up behind it.

It was awesome. But it was also terrifying at the same time.

Jill stood between Wes and Meg. She looked up and down the beach. Red flags dotted the sand, warning everyone to stay out of the ocean.

Not that we need a red flag to tell us that, Jill thought. The huge waves were warning enough.

"Now, this is an ocean you should be afraid of," she said, turning to Meg.

"It's wild, isn't it?" Meg said. She took a deep breath. "It feels wonderful!" she said.

"Wonderful? It doesn't seem wonderful to me," Wes said. "Powerful, maybe. But not wonderful."

"It's so alive!" Meg said.

Jill couldn't believe it. "You're afraid of sitting on a surfboard in a calm ocean, but this doesn't scare you?" she asked.

Meg laughed. "Well, sure, it's scary, but I'm not going in it, am I? It's just so cool to watch!" she explained.

Jill shook her head, smiling. Meg did have a point. There was something incredible about the wind and the sound of the waves and the splattering of rain that was starting.

Meg grinned. Jill grinned back, but then Meg's smile turned to a frown. Jill turned to see what Meg was looking at.

A boy was running down the beach.

Jill recognized Cal's blue swim trunks, even though he was still too far away to see his face clearly. Something about the way he was running and waving his arms made her stomach drop.

Something was wrong.

Jill began sprinting toward him. Meg followed her. When he saw Jill and Meg start running, Wes followed them.

"What is it?" Jill asked when she got close to Cal. "What happened?"

"It's Abby and Sara," Cal said, panting.

"What do you mean?" Meg asked.

"You've got to come help," Cal said. He took a huge breath. "They're in the ocean, and we can't get them to come out!"

Chapter 9 ›
STUPID!

"Are they hurt or anything?" Jill asked.

Cal shook his head. "No, but the warning flags are up everywhere. We keep waving and yelling at them, but it's like they don't get it."

"That was so stupid!" Jill said. She turned to Cal. "Cal, run back to the camp and tell Krista where we are. I don't want to get Abby and Sara in trouble, but I also don't want them to get hurt."

Cal nodded and took off down the beach.

"Come on!" Jill said to Wes. The three of them jogged back the way Cal had come. Soon, Jill saw a small crowd gathered on the beach.

"I bet they're not here to watch the waves," Meg said.

Jill looked from the crowd to the ocean. Sure enough, Abby and Sara were out there. The water was so rough she could only catch glimpses of them. She saw Sara's blond head. Then she spotted Abby's bright pink bathing suit.

"What are they thinking?" Jill asked nervously.

"I don't think they are thinking," Wes said.

Jill squinted her eyes. It was hard to see. The rain was starting to fall harder. The waves were whipping into a frenzy.

Jill waved her arms, trying to get the girls' attention.

For a split second, she thought she saw them wave back. Then a wave loomed up in front of the two girls, and they disappeared.

"What should we do?" Meg screamed. It was getting hard to hear over the wind.

Just then, someone on the beach yelled, "Look!"

Jill spun back to look at the ocean. Salt water stung her eyes, but she knew what she saw.

Abby and Sara were both trying to surf on the same wave.

Jill felt like she was watching it all in slow motion. The two girls lay flat on their surfboards. Then both of them swung their legs up and crouched into a stand. Both girls and boards glided effortlessly, almost like a ballet.

And then one of them wobbled, or maybe it was both of them. One second Sara and Abby were high above the waves. The next second, they were crashing into each other.

Jill held her breath. She strained her eyes, trying to see the boards or the girls as they bobbed to the surface. But the ocean was too wild. She couldn't see anything.

And then she did see someone out in the water, but it wasn't Abby or Sara.

It was Meg.

Chapter 10 ›
PARTNERS

"Meg!" Jill screamed. "Meg!"

Meg didn't turn around. Jill watched as Meg's strong arms cut sharp, solid strokes across the ocean. Her body rose and fell with the waves.

Jill ran in after her. Jill was a good swimmer, but under these conditions, she realized Meg had something she didn't.

Confidence. And courage.

Wes dove into the water too. Jill's arms started to get tired as she tried to catch up with Wes and reach Meg.

Suddenly, Wes and Meg were right in front of her. Meg had Abby under one arm, and Wes was holding Sara.

Jill grabbed Abby's other arm to help support her. Abby wasn't unconscious. That was a good sign. But she was obviously in pain. She moaned, and Jill could tell that she would need to see a doctor.

Meg and Jill dragged Abby onto the beach. They laid her gently in the sand.

When Jill looked up, she saw Wes close behind them. Sara's arm was flung over his shoulder.

Sara fell next to Abby. She was coughing and sputtering.

Jill heard sirens in the distance. The ambulances were coming.

Krista ran over to Jill and Meg. "What happened?" she asked. "Who can tell me what happened?"

Jill shook her head, too stunned to speak. Other voices rose around her, explaining what had happened.

Jill turned to Meg, who was kneeling next to her. "I take it back," she gasped.

Meg shivered, and someone put a towel around her shoulders. "Take what back?" Meg asked through chattering teeth.

"You have more confidence and courage than anyone I know," Jill told her.

Meg smiled. She threw her arms around Jill and hugged her. "So do you, partner! So do you!" she said.

Jill hugged Meg back. Then she looked at Abby and Sara. Paramedics were checking them out.

"Do you think they've learned their lesson?" Meg asked.

"I hope so," Jill said.

She looked back at the ocean. Suddenly, the competition didn't seem that important anymore. In fact, it didn't seem important at all.

Jill turned back to Meg. "Let's forget about the competition next week," she said. "It doesn't matter."

"No way!" Meg said. "We're partners, right? We'll give it a shot."

"Only if you want to," Jill said. "It's really no big deal."

"If you can dive into the ocean in the middle of a hurricane, then I can definitely try to stand on a surfboard," Meg said, smiling. "Deal?"

"Deal!" Jill said happily.

The girls helped each other up, and together, they walked down the beach.

ABOUT THE AUTHOR

Lisa Trumbauer is the *New York Times* bestselling author of *A Practical Guide to Dragons*. She's written about 300 books for children, including novels, picture books, and nonfiction books on just about every topic under the sun (including the sun!). She lives in New Jersey with her husband, Dave, two moody cats, and a dog named Blue.

ABOUT THE ILLUSTRATOR

When Tuesday Mourning was a little girl, she knew she wanted to be an artist when she grew up. Now she is an illustrator who lives in Knoxville, Tennessee. She especially loves illustrating books for kids and teenagers. When she isn't illustrating, Tuesday loves spending time with her husband, who is an actor, and their son, Atticus.

GLOSSARY

competition (kom-puh-TISH-uhn)—a contest

confidence (KON-fuh-duhnss)—strong belief in your own abilities

courage (KUR-ij)—bravery

panicked (PAN-ikd)—scared and worried

paramedics (pa-ruh-MED-iks)—people who are trained to give emergency care

postponed (pohst-POHND)—put off until a later time

pummel (PUHM-uhl)—punch or hit

riptide (RIHP-tide)—a strong current flowing away from shore

suspicious (suh-SPISH-uhss)—as though something is wrong

wipeout (WIPE-out)—to fall

TAKING CARE OF YOUR SURFBOARD

Surfboards are expensive, and they need careful maintenance. If they're taken care of properly, they can last for years. Follow these rules to keep your surfboard in great shape!

1. Don't stand your surfboard against a wall. Invest in a bag to keep your board in so that it doesn't get damaged.

2. Have dings or dents repaired. You can buy a repair kit at a surfboard shop. If you need a quick fix, try using duct tape to cover a dent.

3. Try not to leave your board in the sun. The hot rays can melt the wax and damage your board.

4. Wax helps your feet stay on the surfboard, so make sure that your board always has the proper amount of wax.

SURFING WORDS YOU SHOULD KNOW

The words surfers use are a language of their own! Here are a few surfing words that will help you get started in surf culture.

floater (FLOW-tur)—when the surfer rides the top part of the breaking wave

peak (PEEK)—the central point of the wave

radical (RAD-ik-uhl)—how an extreme move on a surfboard is described

take-off (TAKE-off)—when the surfer stands up on the board

tube ride (TOOB RIDE)—when the surfer rides inside a wave. To someone on shore, the surfer is completely hidden until she comes out of the tube of water. The surfer feels like she is covered by a huge tunnel of water!

DISCUSSION QUESTIONS

1. Why do you think Abby and Sara are mean to the other surfers?

2. Why does Wes help Meg learn how to stand on her board? What are some other ideas you have that could have helped Meg?

3. At the end of the book, Meg helps Abby and Sara even though they were mean to her. Have you ever been in a similar situation? What happened?